Girl Wonder
to the
Rescue

Girl Wonder
to the
Rescue

Malorie
Blackman

Illustrated by Jamie Smith

Tamarind

GIRL WONDER TO THE RESCUE
A TAMARIND BOOK 978 1 848 53134 5

First published in Great Britain in 1994 by Victor Gollancz Ltd

This edition published by Tamarind, an imprint of
Random House Children's Publishers UK
A Random House Group Company

This Tamarind edition published 2014

1 3 5 7 9 10 8 6 4 2

Text copyright © Oneta Malorie Blackman, 1994
Illustrations copyright © Jamie Smith, 2014

The Random House Group Limited supports the Forest Stewardship Council® (FSC®),
the leading international forest-certification organisation. Our books carrying the FSC
label are printed on FSC®-certified paper. FSC is the only forest-certification scheme
supported by the leading environmental organisations, including Greenpeace. Our paper
procurement policy can be found at www.randomhouse.co.uk/environment.

MIX
Paper from
responsible sources
FSC® C016897

Set in Bembo MT

RANDOM HOUSE CHILDREN'S PUBLISHERS UK
61–63 Uxbridge Road, London W5 5SA

www.**randomhousechildrens**.co.uk
www.**totallyrandombooks**.co.uk
www.**randomhouse**.co.uk

Addresses for companies within The Random House Group Limited can be found at:
www.randomhouse.co.uk/offices.htm

THE RANDOM HOUSE GROUP Limited Reg. No. 954009

A CIP catalogue record for this book is available from the British Library.

Printed and bound in Great Britain by CPI Group (UK) Ltd, Croydon CR0 4YY

For Neil and Lizzy,
with love as always.

Malorie Blackman has written over sixty books and is acknowledged as one of today's most imaginative and convincing writers for young readers. She has been awarded numerous prizes for her work, including the Red House Children's Book Award and the Fantastic Fiction Award. Malorie has also been shortlisted for the Carnegie Medal. In 2005 she was honoured with the Eleanor Farjeon Award in recognition of her contribution to children's books, and in 2008 she received an OBE for her services to children's literature. She has been described by *The Times* as 'a national treasure'. Malorie Blackman is the Children's Laureate 2013–15.

Contents

The Birthday Box

It was Mum's birthday two and a half months after Christmas. The twins and I put our money together to buy Mum a present. We had just enough money to buy her a scarf and a card.

"It doesn't look like much." Anthony frowned.

"Yeah, not much at all," Edward agreed glumly.

"It's all we can afford," I sighed.

"It's not very big," said Anthony.

"It's not very chunky," complained Edward.

"It should look like *something* when it's wrapped up," Anthony continued. "A scarf is going to look itchy-titchy."

They made it sound like it was my fault!

"So what should I do?" I asked crossly.

"I don't know," Anthony replied. "You're Girl Wonder . . ."

"Well, you two are the Terrific Twins," I replied. "*You* think of something."

So we all spun around and around, not feeling very super at all. We sat on the floor cross-legged, staring at the scarf and trying to think of a way to make it seem bigger and better than it was.

Then I had an extra-giga-brilliant idea.

"Let's wrap it in tons and tons of paper," I said. "Then it'll look big and chunky and more like *something*."

"Good idea," Anthony agreed.

"Not bad," said Edward.

We ran downstairs. Mum was in the kitchen, taking the vacuum cleaner motor to pieces.

"Mum, we need a box," I said.

"A Ginormous box," added Anthony.

"A HUMONGOUS BOX!" Edward said eagerly.

"Why?" asked Mum.

"We want to put your birthday present in it," Anthony told her.

"Oh, I see . . ." Mum said slowly. "If you tell me what you've got me, then I'll be better able to judge what size box would suit you best."

"We got you . . ."

"EDWARD! Don't tell her!" I interrupted quickly. "Mum, you'll have to wait until tomorrow to see what it is."

Mum mumbled something under her breath. It sounded like "worth a try". She looked in the cupboard under the sink.

"There's this box that held my printer paper," Mum suggested, taking a smallish box out from the cupboard.

"That's much too small," Anthony said immediately.

"Yeah, far too small," Edward agreed.

Then Mum fished out a middling-sized box.

"How about this box?" Mum asked. "This box held all the bottles of lemonade and cream soda that we bought from the supermarket before Christmas."

"Still too small." I shook my head.

"Much too small," Anthony said.

"Far too small," Edward agreed.

Mum looked surprised. She straightened up. "The only other box I've got that's larger is the one the vacuum cleaner came in."

"That'll do," I replied.

"Just," Anthony added.

"Only just," said Edward.

"What did you three buy me? A rhinoceros?" Mum frowned.

"You'll have to wait until tomorrow morning to find out," I said.

"Where's the vacuum cleaner box?" Anthony asked.

"In the cupboard under the stairs," Mum replied. "Er . . . would you three like some help wrapping up my present?"

"No, thanks. We can manage," I said.

We got the box out of the cupboard.

"Now, we'll need some special paper to wrap the box with and we'll need some more paper to pad the box," I said.

"Oh? Is my present something that might break if you don't pad the box?" Mum asked.

I hadn't realized she was listening behind us.

"Go away, Mum," I said crossly, my hands on my hips.

"I was only trying to help," Mum muttered, going back into the kitchen.

More like, she was only trying to be nosy!

Mum came out of the kitchen and handed us a whole roll of brown paper. "You can use this to stuff the box and to wrap it," she said.

Anthony, Edward and I took the box

and the brown paper and went upstairs. Half an hour later, we all sat back to admire our work. The box looked terrific! It was a bit of a shame it had only a scarf in it. We'd filled the box with crumpled, rumpled brown paper and put Mum's scarf right in the middle. The outside was brilliantly wrapped in more brown paper. We drew stars and moons and comets and spaceships all over the brown paper and coloured them in. Then we carried the box downstairs.

"There you are, Mum," I said, as we plonked down the box. "This is your birthday present."

"My goodness! What is it?" Mum said. She bent down and shook the box. It didn't make a sound.

"You'll have to wait until tomorrow to find out," Anthony said.

"Yeah, tomorrow morning," said Edward.

"Can't I open it now?" Mum asked, giving it another shake.

"No, you can't. Wait until your birthday tomorrow," I said firmly.

"Oh, all right then," Mum said reluctantly. But she had a strange gleam in her eyes.

That night I dreamed about flying through the air faster than a speeding rocket and leaping over giant trees with just one jump, when I heard a funny-peculiar noise. It woke me up. I listened. The house was very quiet. I wondered if I'd dreamed the noise. Deciding I must have dreamed it, I pulled my duvet up around my ears and snuggled down to go back to sleep.

Then I heard the same noise again. It was the stairs creaking. We were being burgled.

The Birthday Burglar

I sat up, listening in the darkness. I heard another creak from one of the bottom steps. We were definitely being burgled. I got out of bed and tiptoed out of my room. I was scared – so scared – but I was a superhero and we superheroes have to be braver than brave. I went into the twins' room. They were fast asleep. I might have guessed. It would take fifteen planes flying over our house at the same time to wake those two up.

"Come on, you two. Wake up!" I whispered. "We're being burgled, so this is definitely a job for Girl Wonder . . ."

"And the Terrific Twins?" Anthony whispered back, instantly awake. "Isn't this more a job for the police?"

"Definitely a job for Mum or the police," agreed Edward. "Or a grown-up."

"No, I've got a plan," I said.

My brothers got out of their bunk-beds and we whirled and twirled around quickly but quietly, so that the burglar wouldn't hear us. Luckily there was a full moon so we had the moonlight to see by, otherwise the twins would have tripped over their own feet and made all kinds of noise. I whispered my plan to them. Then we crept slowly and silently down the stairs. We got to the living-room. I could hear noises. There was definitely someone in there, trying their best not to make a sound. We got a chair from the kitchen, then crept to the open living-room door.

"Ready, Terrific Twins?" I whispered.

"Ready, Girl Wonder . . ." the Terrific Twins whispered back.

"Go!"

The Terrific Twins pulled the living-room door shut, then I quickly placed the back of the chair under the door handle. I switched on the hall light, because with the living-room door shut, you can't see much in the hall.

"Right then, Mr Burglar!" I called out. "We have you now! And don't even think about getting out through the window, because there are locks on all the windows in the house and the window key is in the kitchen."

The Terrific Twins were jumping up and down now.

"Hooray! We caught a burglar! Hooray!" Anthony shouted.

"All by ourselves." Edward grinned.

"Yippee!"

"Anthony, you go and get Mum. Edward, you watch the door. I'll phone the police . . ."

"Maxine . . . MAXINE! Let me out of here THIS SECOND!"

We stared at the barred living-room door.

"Mum . . . Mum, is that you?" I asked, surprised.

"OF COURSE IT'S ME. OPEN THE DOOR! NOW!" Mum didn't sound too pleased at all.

We were in seriously, serious trouble. Possibly the most seriously serious trouble we'd ever been in. I unlocked the door.

Sparks flew from Mum's eyes.

"What do you three think you're playing at?" Mum asked furiously, her hands on her hips.

"I heard a noise, Mum," I said. "We thought you were a burglar."

"A burglar . . ." Mum spluttered. "If . . . if you thought you'd heard a burglar in this house you should have come to wake me up first, not tackled him by yourselves. And what do you mean by trapping me in the living room?"

"We couldn't let you escape, Mum," Anthony said. "Not when we thought you were a burglar."

Anthony edged past Mum to look in the living room. I think he still couldn't believe there was no burglar.

"Right! No pocket money for a month for any of you," Mum said. "In fact, no pocket money for a year!"

"But Mum . . ." I said, dismayed.

"Wait a minute, Mum. What's the matter with your present?" Anthony asked.

"What? Er . . . nothing." Mum tried to shoo Anthony out of the living room. I sneaked past her to take a look. The wrapping paper of Mum's present was open at the top.

"I . . . I must have tripped over it in the dark and accidentally opened it," Mum said quickly.

We looked at her. Mum had been doing a spot of burgling!

"Come on, Terrific Twins, let's go back to bed," I said.

"But Mum's been opening . . ." Anthony began.

"But look! Mum's present is . . ." started Edward.

"I think you two must have been

dreaming," I said to the Terrific Twins. "Mum wouldn't be so sneaky as to try and open her birthday present before her birthday. Isn't that right, Mum?"

"Absolutely right, Maxine," Mum agreed.

"I mean, Mum warned us against opening our Christmas presents before Christmas Day – remember? So she wouldn't do the same thing herself," I continued.

"Never mind Mum's present! What about our pocket money?" Anthony wailed.

"Yeah, our pocket money!" said Edward, dismayed. "This is all your fault, Maxine. It was your flimsy-floppy-drippy-droopy idea to catch the burglar."

I looked up at Mum.

"Mum, you said . . ." I got no further.

"I never said anything about your pocket money. You three are dreaming!

Now go back to bed!"

"Are you coming too?" I asked Mum.

"Yes, I am. I've had enough excitement for one night. I think we all have," said Mum, shaking her head and yawning.

I stuck down the wrapping paper again on Mum's present and we all went to bed.

The next morning when Mum finally opened her present and found her scarf, she liked it.

"We put it in a big box because it was only a little present," I explained.

"Size has nothing to do with it. Big things aren't the best things just because they're big," Mum said. "I love this scarf. It's so pretty and just the thing for the spring chill."

We all went for a walk to the park so that Mum could try it out. Hooray for spring! We all love the spring!

It means summer's just round the corner.

The Tooth Fairy Mystery

"Ow! Ouch!" My tooth was killing me! My whole right cheek was puffed up like a balloon.

"That does it, Maxine," said Mum. "If your tooth isn't out by tomorrow, I'm taking you to the dentist."

"Ouch! Ow!" My tooth hurt too much to even protest.

"Let me see it, Maxine," said Edward.

I opened my mouth and wobbled my loose tooth very, *very* gently to show him.

"Where? I can't see anything," Edward said.

"I . . . ri . . . th . . ." I said, with my mouth still wide open.

Edward frowned. "I still don't see anything."

I took my finger out of my mouth. "It's right there. It's the tooth I'm wobbling about." I frowned. "Can't you see it?"

Edward moved closer until his nose was practically in my mouth.

"I still don't see it," he complained.

I frowned at him. "What's the matter with your eyes?" I asked.

"Let me see," said Anthony, barging Edward out of the way.

I showed Anthony. He spotted my wobbly tooth immediately.

"When it comes out, put it under your pillow and then you'll get money from the tooth fairy," said Anthony.

"Tooth fairy!" I scoffed. "There's no such thing as a tooth fairy. It's just Mum who puts money under your pillow when you lose a tooth."

"Is it?" Mum smiled. "You think so?"

"I *know* so," I said. "I caught you the last time, Mum – remember?"

"Ah, but that's why I got in touch with the Tooth Fairy Society and asked them to take over the job," said Mum.

"The Tooth Fairy Society?" said Edward.

"Mum's pulling your leg." I laughed.

"No I'm not, Maxine." Mum shook her head. "I won't be putting money under your pillow any more. Your own personal tooth fairy will be doing it from now on."

"I don't believe a word of it," I said.

Mum shrugged. "Suit yourself. But when your tooth falls out and you put it under your pillow, *I* won't be the one swapping it for money."

"Do we have our own personal tooth fairies too?" asked Anthony, his eyes wide.

"Of course." Mum smiled.

"It's not true. It's just Mum who does it," I protested.

But from the look on Anthony's and Edward's faces, it was clear that they believed Mum rather than me.

In a huff, I marched downstairs.

All afternoon as I sat watching telly, I wibbled and wobbled my tooth around.

I turned it to the left and I turned it to the right and I wobbled it back and forth, back and forth. Until at last with a TWORP! it came out of my gum.

By now Mum, Edward and Anthony had come downstairs. Mum gave me some warm, salty water in a glass. "Go upstairs to the bathroom and rinse your mouth out with that," said Mum. "It will kill infections but don't swallow any or it'll make you sick."

I went upstairs to gargle with the salty water. Now my tooth was out, my mouth didn't hurt at all.

That's more like it, I thought to myself.

Then I had an idea. If Anthony and

Edward didn't believe that Mum was the tooth fairy in our house, then I would prove it to them.

"This is a job for Girl Wonder by herself!" I said to my reflection in the mirror. And I sloshed the last of the salty water around and around my mouth before spitting it out. I ran to my bedroom and put the tooth under my pillow before going back downstairs again.

"How are you feeling?" Mum asked.

"Fine!" I grinned. "What time will you be swapping my tooth for money, Mum?"

"I've already told you, Maxine, I don't do that any more," Mum said, smiling.

"Well, I'm going to wait up all night," I told her. "And if my tooth is still under my pillow by tomorrow morning then that will prove that tooth fairies don't exist."

"You'll never stay up all night." Mum

laughed. "You, Maxine, are a girl who likes her sleep!"

And with that, off Mum went to get a glass of orange juice. Now was my chance.

"Terrific Twins, I need your help," I said to my brothers.

"You do?" said Anthony, surprised.

"Why?" said Edward.

"For what?" asked Anthony.

"I want you two to help me look out for this so-called tooth fairy tonight," I whispered to them. "I'm going to prove that Mum and the tooth fairy are one and the same person."

"But why do you need us?" Edward asked.

"Because Mum's right! If I try to keep watch by myself, I'm only going to fall asleep," I replied. "But with your help, at least one of us will always be awake. There's no way Mum can sneak past all three of us."

"I'm not sure about this, Maxine," said Anthony. "I like my sleep too!"

"So do I!" Edward agreed.

"Oh, come on. Do you want to catch Mum in the act or don't you?" I asked, crossly.

"OK, then," my brothers agreed reluctantly, and we all spun around, bumping and bouncing and bashing into each other.

"Right then. Edward, you can hide behind the wardrobe and Anthony, you can hide behind the curtains," I explained.

"And where will you be?" asked Anthony.

"Yeah! Exactly where will you be?" Edward said.

"I'll be in bed, of course," I said. "Where else would I be? We don't want Mum to get suspicious, do we?"

Anthony and Edward frowned at each other.

"How come we get the hardest bit?" asked Anthony.

"Yeah! How come?"

"Because it's my plan," I replied.

Just then Mum came into the room.

"What are you three up to now?" she said, her eyes narrowing.

"You'll see, Mum." I smiled. "You'll see."

Later that night, Anthony stood behind the curtains and Edward stood by the wardrobe, hidden from the door. I sat up in bed, waving my torch about in the darkness.

"How long have we got to stand here?" asked Anthony.

"Yeah! How long?" asked Edward.

"Until we catch Mum or the tooth fairy or both." I yawned.

"My legs are getting tired," said Anthony.

"My eyelids are getting sleepy," said

Edward. "I can hardly keep them open."

"Well, you must," I insisted with another yawn. "I'm just going to lie down here and *pretend* to be asleep so that when Mum comes in, she'll not suspect anything."

I snuggled down under my duvet whilst Edward and Anthony grumbled and moaned about how they always had to do all the hard bits. I struggled to keep my eyes open, I really did, but my pillow was soft and my bed was warm and my whole body was tired. So I thought, I'll just close my eyes – just for a couple of seconds.

The next thing I knew – it was morning! And Edward and Anthony were nowhere in sight. I lifted up my pillow – and there it was. A bright, shiny one pound coin. Rats! Mum must have sneaked in after I'd fallen asleep and Edward and Anthony had gone back to their own bedroom.

I had a shower and went downstairs. Mum was already down there cooking breakfast.

"Morning, Maxine," she said, grinning.

"Morning, Mum," I said glumly.

"What's the matter with you? Didn't the tooth fairy visit?"

"I know you're the tooth fairy, Mum, so don't pretend you're not," I said.

And then Mum said something that completely threw me.

"Maxine, I give you my word that I haven't been in your room since yesterday afternoon," Mum said seriously. "Cross my heart and hope to die."

"But you must have." I frowned. "How did that pound coin get under my pillow, then?"

Mum just shrugged.

I had a long, hard think.

"Well? Have you solved the mystery yet?" Mum laughed.

"I think there are only three ways that money could have got under my pillow . . ." I began.

"Oh yes?"

"I put my tooth under my pillow yesterday afternoon when it came out. So either you guessed that I'd already put my tooth under my pillow and swapped it for the money yesterday afternoon . . ."

"Or?" prompted Mum.

"Or else Anthony and Edward were in on it and they swapped my tooth for the money when I fell asleep last night . . ."

"Or?" asked Mum.

"Or else there really are tooth fairies!" I said.

Mum creased up laughing. "And which theory do you believe?" she asked.

"I'm not sure," I replied. "But one thing I *am* sure about – the next time one of my teeth falls out, I'm going to stay awake all night. All day and all night if I have to, until I solve the tooth fairy mystery!"

"We'll see!" laughed Mum. "We'll see!"

Edward's Accidents

CR-RRUNCH! Edward raced into the kitchen and kicked the dustpan and brush flying.

"Edward! Watch what you're doing," said Mum.

"Sorry, Mum. I didn't see that there," said Edward. "I just came in for an apple."

Edward ran over to the fruit bowl and stretched past the carton of milk on the work surface. SPLOSSSH! He knocked the carton of milk on to the floor. The milk sloshed about everywhere. CRAAASH! Edward knocked most of the fruit out of the bowl. The apples and oranges and plums bounced all over the work surface. Anthony came running in from the garden.

"Edward! What has got into you recently?" Mum asked, her hands on her hips. "All you seem to do these days is have accidents."

"Sorry, Mum." Edward scrambled to catch all the fruit before it fell on the floor.

"I'll help!" said Anthony.

He ran over to help Edward catch the fruit – only Anthony didn't see the milk on the floor. He went flying up in the air, landing with a SMAAACK!

Edward tried to help Anthony get up but he stepped in the milk and PLONNNK! He slipped over, landing with a thud right next to Anthony.

"Are you two all right?" Mum rushed over to them.

"I am. My bottom isn't," pouted Anthony.

I looked at Mum and Mum looked at me and we both burst out laughing.

"When you two have quite finished messing about, you can both put the fruit back in the bowl, get the mop and clean up that milk and change your wet clothes."

"But it'll be Christmas by the time we do all that!" Anthony protested.

"At least," Edward agreed.

"Then the sooner you start, the sooner you'll finish," said Mum.

I grinned and grinned. I couldn't help it. For once the twins were in trouble and I *wasn't*!

"I'll put the fruit back in the bowl. You can mop the floor," said Anthony quickly.

"Oh, all right then," said Edward reluctantly. "Where's the mop?"

He looked round and round the kitchen.

"Edward, you know I keep the bucket and mop in the cupboard under the stairs," said Mum.

"Oh yes, I remember!" said Edward.

And he ran to get them.

"The bucket's not in here," Edward called out.

I went over to him. "What're you talking about? It's right in front of you."

"Huh!" Edward peered into the dark

34

cupboard until his nose was practically touching the bucket. "Oh yeah! I see it now."

Then Edward bent to pick up the bucket. Only he forgot the mop was in it. Before I could even so much as *squeak* to warn him, the mop fell with a THWACK! Right on Edward's head.

"Ouch!" Edward exclaimed. He rubbed his sore head and pulled a face.

"Edward, are you OK?" Mum asked.

Edward nodded, then shook his head, then nodded again. I almost didn't hear Mum's question because Anthony was so busy laughing.

Edward scowled at him, and me, and Mum!

"I'm going to change my trousers," he said. "I'll be right back."

"I'll come with you," said Mum, a deep frown on her face. "Before you get lost in the wardrobe."

As Edward and Mum went upstairs, I turned to Anthony.

"What's the matter with Edward these days?" I asked.

Anthony shrugged. "He's just having a lot of accidents, that's all."

I shook my head. "It's more than that."

"You think so?" Anthony looked worried.

"I know so," I said.

"So what're we going to do about it?" Anthony asked.

"I don't know," I said. "But this is a job for Girl Wonder . . ."

"And the best-looking Terrific Twin!" said my brother, modestly.

And just for a change, Anthony and I did somersaults up and down the carpet instead of spinning around.

"So how are we going to find out what's wrong with Edward?" I asked.

"Hmm! Maybe we could follow him around?" Anthony suggested.

I thought for a moment. "D'you know, that's a good idea!" I said, surprised.

"I do have them sometimes." Anthony sniffed.

"OK, Terrific Twin," I said. "We'll watch him for the rest of the day and see if there's a reason why Edward is suddenly bumping into things and having accidents."

"Right!" said Anthony.

"But we've got to make sure that Edward doesn't see that we're watching him," I said.

"Right!" said Anthony.

"So we'll have to be careful," I said.

"Right!" said Anthony.

"And stop saying 'right'!" I said.

"Left!" said Anthony.

Honestly!

When Edward came downstairs again, Anthony and I helped him to clean up the kitchen. And all the time we kept a very careful eye on him. We studied

everything he did, looking for possible clues. I soon noticed we weren't the only ones who were watching him. I caught Mum looking at him as well.

And there was definitely something

wrong with Edward. It was as if his arms had shrunk! He kept reaching out for things in the wrong place. His hands wouldn't reach far enough and then he'd

stretch out some more. That's why he kept knocking things over. I thought we were being carefully cautious as we watched Edward, but I don't think we were quite carefully cautious enough.

"STOP IT!" Edward suddenly shouted. "You're all watching me. Stop it!"

Edward sniffed and looked very close to tears.

"It's OK, Edward," I said, putting my arm around him. "I've solved the mystery. Your arms have shrunk and you haven't realized it. That's why you're always having accidents."

"My arms haven't shrunk," Edward protested.

"No, that's not right, Maxine," said Anthony. "The reason Edward's knocking things over is because the light in the kitchen isn't bright enough and he can't see what he's doing."

"It's bright enough for the rest of us," I pointed out.

40

"Edward, go and put on your jacket. We're going out," said Mum quietly. "Maxine, Anthony, you can stay with Miss Ree next door until we get back."

"But where are you going?" I asked.

"And why can't we come with you?" asked Anthony.

"Never mind that now," said Mum impatiently. "Get your things together."

And no matter how hard we tried, Mum just wouldn't tell us where she was taking Edward.

We stayed in Miss Ree's house and played cards and Scrabble. Then we helped Miss Ree weed her garden. Anthony was just about to dig up Miss Ree's forget-me-nots when Miss Ree turned round and told him firmly that forget-me-nots were flowers and *not* weeds.

"Where d'you think Mum and Edward have gone?" Anthony asked.

"Don't know. Don't care," I shrugged.

But it was a lie. I was itching to know.

Time crawled by. One hour turned into two and two hours turned into three. At last Miss Ree's doorbell rang. We rushed to the door. It was Mum. Edward was standing hidden just behind her.

"Where were you?"

"What did you do?"

"Where did you go?"

"Why couldn't we go with you?"

"Did you go somewhere nice?"

Anthony and I were full to bursting with questions.

Mum raised a hand. "Edward and I went to get him something he needs. Come on, Edward. Show them what we went out for."

Edward stepped out from behind Mum.

My mouth fell open. Anthony's eyes were as huge as dinner plates. Edward was wearing glasses!

"Edward, you look brilliant," Anthony said. "Mum, can I have some glasses too?"

"No! You don't need them, Edward does," said Mum. "That's why he kept bumping into everything."

"Edward, they really suit you," said Miss Ree, impressed.

"I know!" Edward grinned.

Already his head was so big, it was only a matter of time before his new glasses

snapped in two!

"It was you two who put me on the right track," Mum said to Anthony and me.

"Yeah! I'm short-sighted! Mum realized what was wrong, thanks to your silly-stupid-senseless suggestions," said Edward proudly.

"But our suggestions worked, didn't they? They couldn't have been that silly-stupid-senseless if they helped Mum to find out what was wrong with your eyes," I said smugly.

"Yeah!" agreed Anthony. "It's just a shame Mum couldn't fix your head at the same time!"

Anthony and the Rap Attack

"What's the time, Mum?" I asked, wondering what had happened to our dinner. Mum had given us an apple each to keep us going until our dinner had finished cooking.

"Maxine wants more!
She's big as a door
And wide as the floor
So it's half-past four!" rapped Anthony.
I gave my brother a dirty look.

"Maxine, it's ten past six," sighed Mum.
"Anthony, how much longer are you

going to say everything in rhyme?"

"If I'm a poet,

I've got to show it!

But I won't blow it!

You know it! You know it!" said Anthony.

"Mum, tell him!" said Edward, covering his ears with his hands and pulling a face.

Anthony was driving us all up the wall and on to the roof! For the last three days, all he'd done was talk in rhymes and raps, raps and rhymes. At first it was fun. Now it was getting on every single one of my nerves.

"You're just jealous," grinned Anthony.

"Pinch me, someone! I must be dreaming. I thought I heard Anthony say something that didn't rhyme!" Mum collapsed back on the sofa.

"I just suggest

That I'm the best.

I beat the rest,

So put me to the test!" rapped Anthony.

"How about if I beat you over the head with this cushion?" I scowled at him.

"Mum, tell him!" said Edward.

Mum closed her eyes and put her hand to her temples. She stood up.

"I'm going to my bedroom to read," Mum said very quietly. "And you three are going to stay down here."

"Don't leave us with him," I begged Mum.

"Yeah, you can't leave us alone with him," Edward pleaded.

Anthony started blowing raspberries and patting his cheeks.

"My name's not Freddy,

The dinner isn't ready!

It's got to cook.

Mum's off the hook.

She's going to her bed to read her library book!" Anthony told us.

"I'll see you three when the dinner's ready," said Mum, even more quietly than before.

And before I could even blink, she was out of the room. I looked at Edward. Edward looked at me.

"Maxine, do something. Save me!" Edward put a cushion over his head, bending the corners down to cover his ears.

I turned to Anthony. "If you make up one more rhyme, I'll . . . I'll . . ."

"I'm off to the loo!

But don't worry 'bout that.

'Cause before you know it,

I'll be back!" said Anthony.

And off he went.

"Maxine, do something – *please*," Edward begged me.

"Come on, Edward," I said. "This is a job for Girl Wonder . . ."

"And one of the Terrific Twins who's getting a headache," Edward complained.

We whizzed-whirled around until we fell over.

"What's your plan?" asked Edward.

"I haven't actually got one yet," I admitted.

"Then think of one – fast," Edward ordered.

I thought and thought and thought. And at last a plan leaped into my head. I told Edward, just as Anthony came running down the stairs. Anthony burst into

49

the room, but before he could say a word,
I got in before him.

"Until you stop rhyming . . ." I began.

"Yeah, until you do . . ." said Edward.

Then Edward and I said together:

"We've decided

Not to talk to you."

Anthony frowned at us.

"But there's nothing finer,

Than to be a rhymer . . ." he began.

Edward and I didn't let him finish.
We said again,

"Until you stop rhyming,
Yeah, until you do,
We've decided
Not to talk to you."

"Come on, Edward. D'you fancy playing a video game?" I asked, ignoring Anthony completely.

"Yes, all right," said Edward.

Edward switched on the telly and put our favourite video game into the game console.

"Me first," I said, picking up the controls.

"If you're no good at this
It won't be much fun.
So let me show you,
How it should be done!" said Anthony.

I looked around the room, puzzled. "Funny! I thought I heard something," I said.

"So did I," said Edward. Then he shrugged. "We must be imagining things."

It was really mean, I know, but Anthony was driving us bonkers!

Anthony looked at us.

"Can I play?" he said at last.

I looked at him. "No more rapping or rhyming?" I asked.

"No more rapping or rhyming," Anthony said glumly.

"Thank goodness." Edward breathed a sigh of relief.

"You two just don't appreciate talent," said Anthony.

"If you had any, we'd appreciate it," I answered.

"Hhmm! Well, you'll both be sorry," Anthony told us. "You're going to miss all my rhymes."

Edward and I fell about laughing.

"You must be joking!" we told him.

And we each took it in turns to play our video game. Our plan had worked. We'd finally got Anthony to shut up!

For the rest of the day Anthony was very quiet. I think he missed making up his rhymes. I didn't!

But the very next day, Edward and I were forced to eat our words.

The Zappers!

The next morning, the moment we walked into school, we knew that something was going on. Charlotte, my best friend, dashed over to me.

"Have you heard the news?" she asked.

"What news?" I said.

"There are notices like this all over the school."

```
┌────────────────────────────────────────────┐
│ ●                                         ● │
│                  WANTED                      │
│                                              │
│   Singers, dancers, musicians, magicians     │
│   - calling any and all performers for       │
│   the school talent show - to be held in     │
│              two weeks' time.                │
│                                              │
│   Auditions will be held this lunch time     │
│           in the assembly hall.              │
│                                              │
│       Mrs Kelsey - Headmistress              │
│ ●                                         ● │
└────────────────────────────────────────────┘
```

"Are you going to try for it, Maxine?" Charlotte asked me, very excited.

"I don't know. A talent show . . . That'll be fun," I said.

"Maxine, we must go for it," said Edward, excited. "Wow! A talent show."

"We've got to try," Anthony agreed.

"But what are we going to do?" I said. "Has anyone got any ideas?"

Anthony and Edward shook their heads.

We wandered away from the notice-board and out into the playground.

"I could sing," Edward suggested.

"Only if you want us to get booed off the stage." Anthony wrinkled up his nose.

He was quite right too! Edward sings like a frog with a sore throat! Still, his voice *is* better than mine, so maybe I shouldn't say much!

"How about dancing?" said Anthony. "We could always do a dance."

"Ballet dancing?" I asked, doubtfully.

Anthony and Edward started jumping around, their arms waving about in the air like tree branches in a force twelve hurricane.

"How does this look?" asked Anthony, anxiously.

"Yeah, how does this look?" asked Edward.

"Like we need a few more lessons before we dance for anyone else," I sighed.

"Ballet dancing is hard work," Anthony gasped.

"Maxine, what *are* we going to do?" asked Edward.

So I said, "That is a job for Girl Wonder . . ."

"And the Terrific Twins," said my brothers. And we all did ballet pirouettes and jumps until I landed on Edward's right foot by accident!

Then I had the best idea of my life.

"I've got it." I clapped my hands and waved them in the air over my head. "I've got it! I've got it!"

"What?" said Anthony.

"Got what?" Edward repeated.

"Anthony, you can do one of your rapping rhymes and Edward and I will do the backing vocals and dances. If we practise at break-time, we'll be ready for the auditions at lunch time." I grinned.

"A brilliant idea," said Edward.

"Extra-super-duper brilliant," I agreed.

But Anthony didn't say a word.

"What's the matter, Anthony?" I asked. "Don't you like my idea?"

"You two told me yesterday to stop making up rhymes and raps," Anthony reminded us.

"That was yesterday," I said.

"Yeah, and this is today," Edward added.

"I'm not going to do it," said Anthony. And he walked off!

I looked at Edward and he looked at me and we both ran after Anthony.

"Anthony, what're you talking about?" I frowned. "You have to do it. We haven't got time to practise anything else and you're brilliant at rhyming."

"That's not what you said yesterday," said Anthony. "You said I didn't have any talent."

"No, we didn't . . ." I began, but Anthony wouldn't let me finish.

"You said I didn't have any talent, because if I did you'd appreciate it," Anthony said huffily.

"We do appreciate it, don't we, Maxine?" Edward said.

"Prove it," said Anthony.

"Prove it? How?" I asked.

Then Anthony got a glittering gleam in his eye.

Oh-oh! I thought. Oh-oh! I don't like the look of this.

"I'm not going to make up any more raps or rhymes until you two promise never to ask me to stop doing them . . ." Anthony began.

"We promise," I said.

"Yeah, we definitely promise," Edward agreed.

"And until you both go down on your knees and say I've got lots and lots of talent!"

What could we do? I didn't want to go down on my knees to Anthony but I wanted to audition for the talent show. With Anthony's help I was sure we'd be chosen, but without Anthony . . .

"This is all your fault, Maxine," Edward told me frostily. "It was your dippy-dorky-dozy idea to get Anthony to stop making up rhymes yesterday."

"Edward, you wanted him to shut up just as much as I did," I said.

"I'm waiting." Anthony sniffed, his nose in the air.

Edward and I looked at each other. Slowly we both got down on our knees.

"Dear Anthony, you have got kilo-tons of talent," I said.

"Mega-tons," Edward agreed. "Maxine, what's bigger than mega-tons?"

"Giga-tons!" I replied. "So please say you'll do it."

"Very well, then," Anthony said, at last. "Since you both asked so nicely."

I got to my feet, brushing off my kneecaps.

"I told you that you'd both be sorry and that you'd miss my rhymes," said Anthony smugly.

"Anthony," I said. "Don't rub it in!"

But he did!

All through the morning break, we practised and practised. Anthony came up with all the rhymes we should say, I invented the dance steps and Edward made up all the drum noises.

At last it was lunch time. We watched

some of the other acts whilst we waited for our turn. One boy read out a poem about some clouds. At least five different people played tunes on their recorders. One boy played his violin. Three of the girls from my class had got together and they did an acrobatics show on the stage, which was quite good. Then it was our turn.

"So what do you call your act?" asked Mrs Kelsey, from in front of the stage.

I looked at the twins. They looked at me. We hadn't thought about that bit!

"Hang on a second," I said quickly. Anthony, Edward and I bent in a huddle to discuss it. "We're called the Zappers!" I said at last.

"OK, Zappers." Mrs Kelsey smiled. "Whenever you're ready."

Anthony stepped forward. I was on one side of him, Edward was on the other. Anthony coughed to clear his throat.

I counted out – just like I'd seen them do on the telly. "One, two, one, two, three, four."

And then we began.

Edward started slapping on his puffed-out cheeks. I started drumming on my chest and making rhythmic raspberry noises! We all started dancing, using the steps we'd rehearsed in the playground. Then Anthony began.

"My name is Tony,
You know it's true,
We've got a lot
To say to you.
With my sister, Max,
And my brother, Ed,
If you don't like this
You must be dead!"

I started snapping my fingers whilst Edward took over the drum noises by slapping his chest.

"We're called the Zappers
We're finger-snappers
And great toe-tappers,
We're the youngest rappers!" rhymed
Anthony.

I smiled at him. He'd made up a whole new verse, just like that. What a hero!

Then it was Edward's turn. He stepped forward and started snapping his fingers.

"So don't try to stop us,
Or even top us.

'Cause we won't lose it,

We're busy making music!" rapped Edward.

"We won't cause a scene

We won't make a fuss

If you, Mrs Kelsey,

Will just choose us!" we all said together. "Yeah!"

And with that we all did the splits – well, as close as we could get to them!

Mrs Kelsey and all the others in the hall started clapping and cheering and whistling. I grinned at Anthony and Edward. They beamed back at me.

"You three are definitely going to be in the show!" Mrs Kelsey told us at once. And she hadn't said that to anyone else as soon as they'd finished. She'd told everyone else that they'd get her final decision by the end of the day.

"For once, one of your dizzy-dopey plans actually worked, Maxine," said Edward, amazed.

"Thanks to Anthony, the most supreme, the most excellent rapper in the universe!" I grinned.

And I meant it too!

Looking After Thunder

It was raining. I don't mean just a spot of water here and a drop of water there – I mean it was *pouring*. As if the clouds were just huge, bottomless buckets of water which were being tipped over us. The twins and I were hurrying along the road after school, desperate to get home.

"I'm soaked," said Edward, coughing and spluttering as some water ran into his mouth.

"I bet I'm more soaked than you," said Anthony.

"Well, I couldn't be more wet if I

jumped in a swimming pool," I said, rubbing the rain-water out of my eyes so I could see where I was going.

Then I heard a strange sound. I stopped walking.

"Edward, Anthony, did you hear that?" I frowned.

My brothers stopped walking and listened too. There it was again. A strange, whimpering noise. And it was coming from behind a horse-chestnut tree in the park beside us.

"Edward, go and see what's making that noise," I said.

"You go!" Edward told me.

"Go on then, Anthony. Don't be a chicken," I said, trying to persuade my other brother.

"No way! I'm not going by myself. It might be anything," said Anthony.

I sighed. "Then I reckon that this is a

job for Girl Wonder . . ."

"And the sopping-wet Terrific Twins," said Anthony.

"The dripping-wet Terrific Twins," Edward agreed.

And we all jumped up and down in the puddle we were standing in, to activate our superhero powers.

"Right then. We'll all go," I said, once we'd finished leaping up and down.

"You first," said Anthony.

"Yeah, you first and me last! I'll stay

here and act as a look-out," said Edward.

"Maxine, *anything* could be making that noise," began Anthony. "It could be . . ."

"Shush!" I whispered, my finger over my lips. "We don't want to scare it off, whatever it is."

"We don't?" Anthony asked.

"We don't," I said firmly.

We all looked around but no one was near. Anthony and I crept across the wet muddy ground towards the horse-chestnut tree, where the noise was coming from. We crept around the tree – and then we saw it. A tiny puppy in a soggy, soaking-wet cardboard box. The puppy's fur was so wet it looked like a baby beaver or otter which had just climbed out of a river.

I picked up the puppy which was too weak to even stand up in my hands. It only had the strength to whimper and sniffle softly as I held it.

"What are we going to do with it?" Anthony asked.

"We're going to take it home," I said firmly, walking back to the main road.

"But Mum said we can't have a dog – remember?" Anthony reminded me. "She's said that hundreds and hundreds of times."

"We can't just leave it there," I said. "It'll die if we just leave it there."

Already its eyes were closing. I could feel that the puppy was breathing, but it was so still it scared me.

"Come on, you two," I said.

And without saying another word, we ran all the way home.

"Mum, Mum!" I called out as soon as we got home.

Mum came flying out of the living room. "Oh no you don't, you three! Take off your wellies and your coats and scarves and hats right there, before you go dripping water all through the house."

"Mum, we heard a strange noise when we were coming home from school . . ."

"And so we went to have a look . . ."

"And we found a puppy in a cardboard box . . ."

"And the puppy was all wet and cold . . ."

"And we couldn't leave it . . ."

We all spoke at once whilst I held out

my hands to Mum, to show her what we'd found.

"Maxine, what's going on?" Mum frowned.

We all tried to tell her again what happened, but Mum put one hand up.

"One at a time. Maxine, you start."

"We found him in the storm, Mum . . ." I began. And very slowly, very carefully, I told Mum exactly what had happened.

"So we couldn't just leave him there, could we, Mum?" I said.

Edward, Anthony and I all held our breath as we waited for Mum to answer. She looked at each of us in turn and then down at the puppy.

"No, of course you couldn't," she smiled at last. "Bring him into the kitchen."

We followed Mum into the kitchen where she got out a cardboard box she'd used to carry home the shopping.

"Anthony, get me some old newspapers from the living room. Edward, run upstairs and get me an old towel. I'll warm up some milk on the cooker," said Mum.

For the next half an hour we were all busy. We lined the box with newspapers until it was very soft and warm. Then Mum very carefully dried our puppy's fur.

"This towel is just for the puppy from now on," Mum told us.

Then we poured out some warm milk into a saucer. But although the puppy opened its eyes, it was too weak to stand up and drink.

Mum squatted down over the puppy, a

deep frown on her face. She very gently stroked its fur.

"Aren't you pretty? As you were found in a thunderstorm, we should call you Thunder," Mum said gently. "Come on then, Thunder. You have to drink your milk if you want to get better."

I looked at Mum. Thunder was the perfect name for our puppy. I looked at our puppy again. It looked so weak.

"Don't let our puppy die, Mum." Anthony sniffed.

"Yeah, don't let it die." Edward shook his head.

"Edward, go and wash out one of my rubber gloves over there by the sink – inside and out," Mum said.

Edward ran over to the sink and did just that. Then Mum poured the rest of the warm milk from the saucepan into her glove. As we watched, she carefully pricked a small hole in one of the fingers of the glove. Then she came over to our puppy. Mum squeezed the glove finger until some of the milk dribbled out and ran along the puppy's lips. Thunder's tongue snaked out to lick up the milk.

"Hooray!" we all shouted.

"Not so fast." Mum shook her head. "We've still got a long way to go yet."

Mum squeezed out some more milk. Thunder licked that up as well. Then Mum held the finger of the rubber glove over Thunder's mouth. I held my breath, waiting anxiously to see if Thunder would feed. He licked the finger of the rubber glove once. And again. Then he lifted his head slightly and began to suck on the finger. The twins and I danced around the kitchen. Thunder was feeding!

"As soon as he's better and able to stand on his feet, I'll call the RSPCA," said

Mum. "They'll be able to take him away and look after him."

I froze. So did Anthony and Edward. We stared at Mum.

"Oh please, Mum. We can't give Thunder away," pleaded Edward.

"We have to look after him. We found him," added Anthony.

"We rescued him, Mum. We can't give him away now," I begged.

Mum looked at us. "Small, cute puppies grow up very quickly into huge dogs. They need to be fed and watered and walked regularly. Are you three prepared to do that?"

"Yes, we are."

"We promise."

"We'll walk him every day," we said quickly.

"Pets aren't for a week or a month, they're for life. And they're a lot of

responsibility," said Mum, sternly.

"We've got a lot of responsibility," said Anthony.

"Yes, tons of it," Edward agreed.

"We'll be responsible, Mum. We'll take it in turns to feed Thunder and walk him and look after him – for ever and ever. We promise," I begged.

Anthony and Edward nodded vigorously, agreeing with my promise.

"Please, Mum. *Please* . . ."

"All right then," Mum said at last.

"Yippee!"

"Hooray!"

"Not so fast," said Mum. "I'm still phoning the RSPCA first thing in the morning. If Thunder really has been abandoned then you can keep him, but only if you all keep your promise."

And we ran and danced and leaped and jumped about so much that by the time we'd finished our clothes were almost dry again!

"Thanks, Mum," we said, grinning. We

all hugged her tight, tight, tight.

At last, we had a proper pet! A pet that could do a bit more than swim about and eat, which was all our goldfish Bugsy ever did! We had our very own dog called Thunder.

"Welcome to our family, Thunder," I said.

"You're going to love it here," said Edward.

"And we're going to take such good care of you," said Anthony.

Thunder raised his head slowly and looked at us. And do you know – I'm sure he smiled!

So once again it was Girl Wonder and the Terrific Twins to the rescue. Isn't it always!

Have you read
these other books about

Girl Wonder
and the
Terrific Twins?

Girl Wonder's Winter Adventures

Malorie Blackman

Children's Laureate 2013-2015

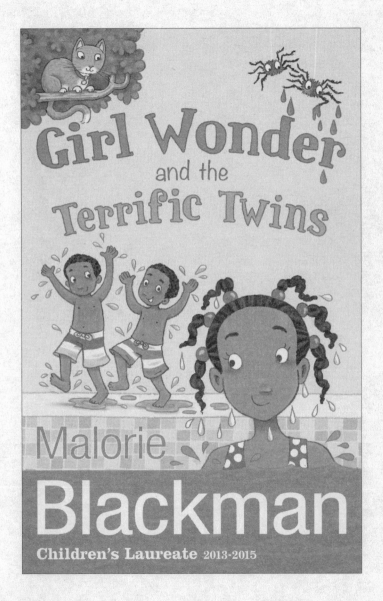

Girl Wonder
and the
Terrific Twins

Malorie
Blackman

Children's Laureate 2013-2015